Riding the Skateboard Ramps

Story by Annette Smith
Illustrations by Richard Hoit

Zac and Grandad had just arrived at the new skateboard park.

"Look!" said Grandad. "Matt and Lucy from next door are here."

"Matt is **so** good at skateboarding," said Zac, as they watched Matt riding up and down the ramps. "I wish I could do tricks like that."

Matt rode over and jumped off his board. "Hi, Zac. Hi, Mr Hill," he said. "Lucy and I are practising for the display next Saturday."

"It's the official opening of this new park," said Matt's sister, Lucy, coming over to join them. "There's a special event for the under ten-year-olds. Why don't you come in it, Zac?"

Zac wasn't sure that he wanted to go in a display. "I'm not really good enough," he said, "because I don't even know how to ride the ramps yet. I only know how to go backwards and forwards, and how to turn my board."

"That's okay. You just need some more practice," said Matt. "When you get really good, I'll show you how to do a kick-flip like this!" he added, as he pushed off. He made it look easy as his board rolled part way up the ramp. Then with a flick, he flipped his skateboard over, crouching slightly as he landed back on top of it.

Matt showed Zac and Lucy some easier moves, and then he left them to practise by themselves. They were concentrating so hard that they didn't notice that a girl was watching them.

After a while, Zac and Lucy propped their skateboards against the fence, and went over to watch Matt. He was doing jump moves over some rails.

Grandad walked around to the far side of the big ramp, because he wanted to check some seats and railings. Grandad was an engineer, and he had helped to design the new park.

Suddenly, the girl who had been watching them grabbed one of the skateboards! She pushed off quickly, and the board rolled down the ramp. But she was going too fast, and she lost control. She let out a yell as she tumbled backwards.

Zac spun around. "Hey, are you all right?" he called.

The girl stood up quickly, and muttered something that they couldn't hear.

"That girl's skateboard looks just like mine!" exclaimed Zac.

Lucy looked across to where they had left their boards. "Where's your board, Zac?" she asked. "I can only see mine!"

"I left it beside yours," said Zac, looking puzzled.

"Do you think that girl has taken it?" whispered Lucy.

"I'm not sure," said Zac. "Should we go and ask her?"

Lucy nodded, and they went over to where the girl was skating.

"Hi!" said Zac to the girl. "I left my board over by the fence. Did you borrow it?"

The girl ignored them as she whizzed past. Zac and Lucy didn't know what to do.

Just then, an older boy came running towards them. "Jaimie! I've been looking everywhere for you," he shouted. "Whose board is that anyway?"

The girl didn't answer.

The boy looked at Zac and Lucy. "Is that your board?" he asked them. "Did my sister ask you if she could borrow it?"

Zac shook his head. He was beginning to feel uncomfortable.

Jaimie flew past them and called out to her brother defiantly, "I **really** want to learn how to skate properly. I wouldn't have to take other people's boards if you weren't so mean. You never let me use any of yours!"

"That's no excuse, Jaimie," said the boy crossly. "You can't just **take** other people's things like that!"

Matt came over to see what was happening. "Hey!" he said, recognising the older boy at once. "You're Kurt Harrison, aren't you? I've seen you riding the ramps! You're the best! Everyone will be watching you at the display on Saturday."

The boy grinned. "Thanks," he said.

As Jaimie listened to them, she began to feel bad about taking Zac's skateboard. "I suppose I should have asked you if I could borrow your board," she said, as she handed it back to Zac.

"Yes, you should have," said Kurt. "But if you want to learn to skate so badly, I'll go back home and get some of my gear. Then I'll show you how to ride the ramps properly."

In no time at all, Kurt was back at the park with skateboards and some safety gear. Everyone admired Kurt's skill as he rode up and down the ramps. He went slowly at first, demonstrating how to twist and turn the board in different directions. Then he showed them some of his best tricks.

For the next hour, Zac and the others practised hard. Kurt was a great teacher, and Jaimie started to feel much happier.

Grandad had been watching and listening. "You're all doing really well," he called. "That looks like so much fun!"

Grandad and Kurt cheered as Zac rode up the ramp in front of them and turned to ride back down again.

"I can't believe that this is so easy," shouted Zac, as he rolled along at great speed. "I'm going to enter that display after all!"